Hello, Reader!

Two crazy pigs lived on
Mr. and Mrs. Fenster's farm.
They tickled the hens while they were laying eggs.
They tied the cows' tails together while they were
giving milk.
"Stop that, you crazy pigs," yelled Mr. Fenster.

Laugh along with these TWO CRAZY PIGS!

To Ian M. Nagel,
with love and thanks for all your ideas.
—K.B.N.

For Robin
—B.S.

Copyright © 1992 by Karen Nagel.
Illustrations copyright © 1992 by Brian Schatell.
All rights reserved. Published by Scholastic Inc.
CARTWHEEL BOOKS is a trademark of Scholastic Inc.
HELLO READER! is a registered trademark of Scholastic, Inc.
Library of Congress Cataloging-in-Publication Data
Nagel, Karen.
    Two crazy pigs / by Karen Nagel; illustrated by Brian Schatell.
        p.   cm. — (Hello reader)
    "Cartwheel Books."
    "Level 2 ."
    Summary: Two pigs who drive the farmer and his wife crazy with their silliness and pranks decide to move to a new farm, only to be missed by all when they leave.
    ISBN 0-590-90759-X
    [1. Pigs—Fiction.   2. Domestic animals—Fiction.]   I. Schatell, Brian, ill.   II. Title.   III. Series.
PZ7.N1345Tw   1992
[E]—dc20   91-18860
                                                                            CIP
                                                                            AC

19 18 17 16 15 14   7 8 9/9 0/0 24
                        Printed in the U.S.A.
                First Scholastic printing, April 1992

Two Crazy Pigs

by Karen Berman Nagel
Illustrated by Brian Schatell

SCHOLASTIC INC.
New York Toronto London Auckland Sydney

We are two crazy pigs.
We lived on the
Fenster farm.

We tickled the hens while
they were laying eggs.

"Stop that, you crazy pigs,"
yelled Mr. Fenster.

We tied the cows' tails together while they were giving milk.

"Stop that, you crazy pigs,"
yelled Mrs. Fenster.

Instead of rolling in the mud,
we threw it at each other.

OOPS!

"Pack your bags and leave!"
yelled Mr. and Mrs. Fenster.

All the animals cried, "We'll miss you, crazy pigs!"

We went down the road to
Mr. and Mrs. Henhawk's farm.
"Do you have room here for
two crazy pigs?" we asked.

Mr. Henhawk made us a new
pigpen.

He laughed when we dipped
the sheep's tail in ink.

Mrs. Henhawk let us make
mud pies in her stove.

One day the Fensters' cow,
Shirley, came to visit.

"Will you come back to the
farm?" Shirley asked.

"The hens are not laying eggs.

The cows have stopped
giving milk."

"No," we said. "Mr. and
Mrs. Henhawk love us for
who we are — crazy pigs."

We pulled Shirley's tail and
said good-bye. Then she went
back to the Fenster farm.

One week later, all of the
Fensters' animals came to
the Henhawk farm.

Shirley spoke.
"The Fensters have moved to the city. Do you have room for us here?"

Mr. and Mrs. Henhawk asked all the animals to live on their farm.

We were very happy to have our friends back.

We rubbed everybody's faces in mud.

We jumped on the Henhawks'
feather bed for two hours.

We were so happy! "Let's visit the Fensters in the city for old time's sake," we said.

"Are you kidding?" asked
Shirley.
"Are you sure?" asked
Mr. Henhawk.

"No," we said, "we're crazy!"